The Children's Moon

BY

CARMEN AGRA DEEDY

ILLUSTRATED BY

JIM LaMARCHE

SCHOLASTIC PRESS   NEW YORK

There once was a time

when the sun alone ruled the day,

the moon graced the night,

and little children were put firmly to bed before sunset.

But one dawn, as the moon slipped out of the sky, she heard

laughter. It was high and sweet, like the daintiest of silver bells.

She paused. "What is that sound?"

"Hurry!" The sun urged her along. "The children are waking,

and it's my turn to shine."

So the moon glided away

in a shimmering trail of moondust.

That dusk, when they met again, the moon could scarcely contain herself.

"Oh, do — do — *do* tell me about the children, won't you?"

"Surely you've seen them," huffed the sun.

"Only by moonlight," she reminded him.

"Well," said the sun, "they are small and fast — and make a great deal of noise. But they *do* love drawing pictures of me."

"They never see *me*," sighed the moon.

"Unless you'd let me come out by day?"

"Certainly not!" snapped the sun.

"You know the rules."

"The day is mine.

The night is yours."

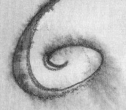

"A pity," said the moon. "I've often wondered how the world would look aglow in your golden rays."

This last comment seemed to please him.

He wasn't a bad fellow, you see.

Just so very grand and, well, *brilliant*.

And so, the sun told the moon of a world
of fierce light and vibrant colors.

Of glittering lakes, misty jungles,
and herds of animals
that flowed like water
across endless savannahs.

He described waking rivers that stretched to the sea,

gleaming cities and the people who toiled in them,

and bees abuzz with their own industry.

Last, he told her of adoring sunflowers that

followed his every move across the sky.

"And that," he said, "is the world by day."

Before the moon

could speak,

the sun had vanished.

The following dawn, the moon couldn't wait to see her friend. As he passed, she called after him.

"Would you like to know how the world looks by night?"

"No, I would not," groaned the sun, "but I can see that you are determined to tell me."

With delight, she told him about moonflowers and the ribbonlike aurora borealis.

She described screech owls and bats.

She waxed joyful as she spoke of fireflies,

and seas aglow with plankton — until

she realized her friend was no longer listening.

"Yet, the most wondrous of all are the stars."

At once, the sun's interest flickered.

"Wait — what? Stars, you say?"

"Oh," said the moon, as if it was now of little

interest to her. "Stars are suns, just like you."

"PREPOSTEROUS!"

he shouted. "Wouldn't I have seen these other suns?"

"Would you?" The moon's tone was kind.

"Oh. My light chases away the night. I can't see them."

The poor sun seemed quite undone.

"Of course," said the moon, "there is a way.

But we'd have to work together."

And as the moon gently eclipsed

her friend, the sun saw —

not a thousand, nor a million,

nor a billion, nor a trillion —

but a universe of countless stars!

Suns, much like himself:

some dying,

some newly born.

And if he felt less grand . . .

he also felt a little less lonely.

"Thank you," the sun whispered.

"Now," sang the moon, "will you please-please-*please*-with-a-comet-on-top let me see the children?"

The sun nodded his fiery head. "Of course. But it's a poor trade, my friend. I've seen the stars."

A sudden thought turned the moon quite blue.

"How will the children see me, with *you* in the sky?"

"Because I will shine on you as never before," vowed her friend.

And as the moon's light grew bold, and bolder still,

she heard a sound . . . like the daintiest of silver bells.

And the children, whose small faces shone like stars . . .

were *moonstruck*.

"May I come again?" whispered the moon.

"They'd never forgive me if you didn't," replied her friend.

And that is why when she appears by day — when even the youngest child is awake to see her — she is called . . .

The Children's Moon.

MORE ABOUT THE MOON

If you want to see "the children's moon," you can plan it!

The moon appears just before — and just after — it phases into a full moon.

    1. To see it in the afternoon, start looking to the sky about a week *before* it waxes into a full moon.

    2. To see it in the morning, start looking for it the week *after* it wanes from a full moon.

    3. And remember, on those days each month when you can't see the moon by day, it (and the stars) are still there!

To find out when the next full moon is scheduled to appear, check here:

https://catalina.lpl.arizona.edu/moon/phases/calendar

It's Just a Phase

It takes 29.5 days, and many phases, for the moon to go from New Moon to New Moon.

Each phase has its very own lovely name. When the moon appears bigger, we say it is waxing.

When it appears to grow smaller, we say it is waning.

New Moon   Waxing Crescent   First Quarter   Waxing Gibbous   Full Moon   Waning Gibbous   Third (or Final) Quarter   Waning Crescent

Strange & Wonderful Facts about the M●●n

Human beings have been fascinated with the moon since the dawn of time. The moon is shrouded in mystery and, for that reason, myths and legends abound — but these moon facts are almost as good as any story.

● The moon does not only reflect the sun's light! It *does* radiate light — just not at a wavelength we can see! How about that?

● The earth's gravity is what gives the moon its rotational speed. Since the earth and the moon are at the right size and distance from each other, earthlings only ever see one side of the moon. Unless you're lucky enough to be an astronaut, of course!

● The moon's gravity is 1/6th of that of the earth, but it's enough to make the oceans bulge when they face the moon. This is what makes high tides. The larger the moon is in the sky, the stronger its pull on the ocean waters.

● The moon isn't a sphere (a ball). Rather, it's slightly egg-shaped, with one of the ends pointed toward earth. Cool, right?

● The sun, moon, and earth must all line up in order to create a lunar or solar eclipse.

● The moon never actually turns blue. But when there are two full moons in the same calendar month, we call the second one a Blue Moon. And when we say "once in a blue moon" we mean something that rarely happens. (Even though a blue moon happens regularly — every two years or so!)

● There are moon trees. Okay, not really. But in 1971, astronaut Stuart Roosa took tree seeds into space. They circled the moon with him thirty-four times. Some of those seeds were planted on earth and are called moon trees. Their offspring are called — you guessed it — half-moon trees!

● There is no proof that the moon is made of cheese. (Just making sure you're still paying attention!)

To learn more about the moon, go to: https://spaceplace.nasa.gov/search/moon/

To my grandchildren, Ruby, Sam, Grace, Brady, and Chloe. —C.D.

For Charlotte. —J.L.

Special thanks to Janice del Negro. — C.D.

With gratitude to Jackie Faherty, Astrophysicist at the American Museum of Natural History, for her expert read of the back matter text.

Moon phases: Designed by Freepik.

Library of Congress Cataloging-in-Publication Data

Names: Deedy, Carmen Agra, author. | LaMarche, Jim, illustrator.
Title: The children's moon / by Carmen Agra Deedy ; iIllustrated by Jim LaMarche. Description: First edition. | New York : Scholastic Press, an imprint of Scholastic Inc., 2021. | Audience: Ages 4–8. | Audience: Grades K–1. | Summary: One dawn the moon hears the laughter of children waking up and she yearns to see them, but the day belongs to the sun and he will not trade places; so the moon tempts him with stories of the stars and the two come up with a compromise that explains why the moon can sometimes be seen in the daytime.
Identifiers: LCCN 2020042723 | ISBN 9781338216394 (hardcover)
Subjects: LCSH: Moon—Juvenile fiction. | Sun—Juvenile fiction. | Friendship—Juvenile fiction. | CYAC: Moon—Fiction. | Sun—Fiction. | Friendship—Fiction.
Classification: LCC PZ7.D3587 Cj 2021 | DDC 813.54 [E]—dc23

10 9 8 7 6 5 4 3 2 1   21 22 23 24 25

Printed in China   38
First edition, October 2021

Jim LaMarche's illustrations were created with acrylics and pencil on Arches watercolor paper. ★ The text type was set in Adobe Garamond Pro. ★ The display type was set in Absalom WF. ★ The book was printed on 157gsm FSC Golden Sun matte paper and bound at RR Donnelly Asia. ★ Production was overseen by Catherine Weening. ★ Manufacturing was supervised by Shannon Rice. ★ The book was art directed and designed by Marijka Kostiw and edited by Dianne Hess.